T0165246

Shaping Little Minds
for the Future

**Elnora Holloway and
Connie Lamb**

authorHOUSE®

AuthorHouse™
1663 Liberty Drive
Bloomington, IN 47403
www.authorhouse.com
Phone: 1-800-839-8640

First published by AuthorHouse 6/23/2009

ISBN: 978-1-4389-7277-0 (sc)

Printed in the United States of America
Bloomington, Indiana

This book is printed on acid-free paper.

Table of Contents

Obedience Pays

(Based on Genesis 2:15 – 3:19)

In the beginning of time God created the first man whose name was Adam. Later God decided to make Adam a helper, the first woman, her name was Eve. God placed Adam and Eve in a beautiful garden which was called the Garden of Eden. They were placed there to enjoy God's beautiful creation of trees, flowers and other plants. Not only were the trees beautiful to look at, some of them produced tasty fruit.

The tree of the knowledge of good and evil was located in the middle of the garden. Adam and Eve had been given special instruction to eat from any of the trees except of the one in the middle of the garden.

Adam and Eve sampled the fruit from all the other trees. Their curiosity was aroused when an old serpent came along to deceive Eve. With his smart voice, he asked Eve if God had said do not eat from any of the trees? Even told the serpent God said enjoy the fruit from all the trees except the one in the middle of the garden, or they would "surely die". The serpent said again in his smart voice – "You will not surely die; God just knows you will be as smart as He is if you eat from that tree." Eve was really curious now!

Eve decided to try some of the fruit – it was good, so she gave some to Adam. Immediately Adam felt ashamed, naked, and guilty. He exclaimed, "Oh Eve, we have disobeyed God!"

When God appeared in the evening He said, "Adam where are you?" Adam replied, "I am hiding because I am naked." God said, "How do you know you are naked? Did you eat from the tree in the middle of the garden?" Adam said, "Eve gave the fruit to me and I ate it." Eve said, "The serpent fooled me and I ate it." Adam, Eve, and the serpent had to suffer the consequences for this great act of disobedience.

God told the serpent he would have to crawl on its belly and eat dust from now on. He told Adam he would have to work hard and grow his food. Eve would have pain during child birth. This punishment was passed down to all generations just because Adam and Eve failed to obey in the garden.

There are always consequences for every action. When you obey, you are rewarded with good things. Disobedience brings punishment, guilt and shame.

Discussion Questions

1. What does the word consequences mean?

2. Who should you obey?

3. Who/what is our serpent?

4. Which voice should you obey

Activity #1

Use yellow construction paper to make happy/sad faces. Cut out a circle three inches in diameter for each child. On one side of the circle have children draw features for a happy face. Draw features for a sad face on the other side. Attach the happy/sad face to a Popsicle stick or tongue depressor then read the following statements: Show the happy face when the statement describes obedience, show the sad face when the statement describes disobedience.

    a. Always do as you are told.

    b. Tell lies

    c. Ride your bike in the street

    d. Always tell the truth

    e. Talk back to parents, teachers and other adults

    f. Share with your friends

Activity #2

Play Simon Says – Instruct children to only do what Simon says. If they do something that Simon did not say, they are out of the game. Play the game long enough for the children to get the concept of obedience. Command suggestions are as follows:

Clap your hands, Walk in place, wave good-bye, Give me a smile, Stamp your foot, rub your head, Close your eyes, nod your head, turn around, sit down

"Blessed are the pure in heart, for they shall see God"
(Matthew 5:8)

Jesus Taught from the Mountainside

(Based on Matthew 5:1-11)

Would you like to be happy? One beautiful day Jesus sat down on the side of a huge grass covered mountain and began to teach His disciples how to be happy. A large crowd of other people wanted to hear how to be happy too so they gathered around and listened. Jesus was a great teacher and he taught many good lessons about living with one another. Even though this was a long, long time ago, we can still do the things Jesus taught to be happy.

He said we can be happy when we have a good attitude. Attitude is the way we feel or act toward something or someone. We need to always think about good things. We should always build others up and not be selfish. We should even be nice to those boys and girls that are not nice to us. When we remember to do these things we can be happy almost always.

Jesus said that we would be sad sometimes. But He also said that he would never leave us alone, so we must remember when we feel sad Jesus is right there by our side. We must also remember to do all the things Jesus taught if we want to be happy. When we do these things Jesus is happy and we can look to live with Him one day.

Discussion Questions

1. What are some things Jesus taught us to do to be happy?

2. Who can help us to learn and do what Jesus taught?

3. What does the word attitude mean?

Activity 1

Make a copy of the following statements for each child. Have the children draw a happy face beside the statement that makes Jesus happy and a sad face beside the statement that would not make Jesus happy.

1. Clean up your room when you are told
2. Pick a fight with a classmate
3. Share your toys or snacks with a friend
4. Tell a lie to cover some bad act
5. Come when mom or dad calls
6. Give someone a hug
7. Cheat while playing games
8. Make a mess and leave it for mom to clean up

Activity 2

Happy Mountain Climbing

Use brown poster paper to make a mountain shape. Divide it into four sections. Cut out four rocks for tags. Write these words on the rocks: SHARING, LOVING, HELPING, and CARING. Place one rock on each section of the mountain. Let children write sentences to demonstrate each word and place in the proper section of the mountain.

"My sheep hear my voice, and I know them, and they follow me."
(John 10:27)

Follow the Good Shepherd

(Based on John 10)

The Good Shepherd leads sheep to greener pastures. In the Bible, Jesus is known as the Good Shepherd. Jesus is God's only son and he wants him to lead his sheep to greener pastures, obedience, honesty, and humility. We are his sheep.

Jesus compared his disciples to sheep. Sheep are animals that need to be led to good food, water and a place to rest. Jesus knew his disciples needed to be led also. Sheep are usually led by a shepherd. When Jesus compared his sheep, he appointed himself to be their shepherd. The sheep get to know their shepherd, and will follow him wherever he leads them. The disciples got to know Jesus and followed him wherever he led them. He was always looking for them and taking care of their needs. When they needed good food, water, and rest, he led them to the right place. Sometimes some of the sheep would get distracted and stray away from the other sheep and their good shepherd that takes care of them. When one strays he comes in contact with the bad shepherd. The bad shepherd doesn't care for the sheep. He allows them to get in trouble.

As children of God, Jesus is our shepherd. As long as we follow him, he will lead us to good things. We will have good thoughts, good attitudes and good habits. But when we stop following the things Jesus taught, we are like the sheep that strayed away and followed the bad shepherd. The bad shepherd leads us in the wrong way. The wrong way leads to disobedience, ugly attitudes, mean thoughts, and almost always get us in trouble.

We must choose to follow the good shepherd. Jesus is the good shepherd. He always leads us to greener pastures. Greener pastures mean the better things in life. So follow the good shepherd.

Discussion Questions

1. Who is the good shepherd?

2. Where does the good shepherd lead us?

3. What kinds of things do we experience when we don't follow the good shepherd?

Activity 1

Have children demonstrate following the good shepherd by role playing. Example situations:

1. Child obeying parent (obedience)

2. Finding and returning an item that is lost (honesty)

3. Befriending a new boy/girl at school or church (humility)

Activity 2

Make an edible sheep

You will need a bag of large marshmallows and a bag of stick pretzels. Give each child two marshmallows, and six pretzels. Instruct them to turn one marshmallow hamburger style for the body, turn the other one hot dog style for the head, use a pretzel and join the two. Put four pretzels in the bottom of the body and add one pretzel at the end of the body for the tail. Use small pieces of candy for the facial features.

"And when Jesus came to the place, he looked up and saw him,
and said unto him, 'Zacchaeus, make haste and come down:
for today I must abide at thy house'."
Luke 19:5

Zaccahaeus, Come Down

(Based on Luke 19:1-9)

Would you like to be Jesus' friend? Zacchaeus met Jesus and was quickly changed. When Zacchaeus heard Jesus was traveling Jericho, he made plans to see him. Zacchaeus was a very important man in Jericho. He was tax collector. He was very short in stature. The streets of Jericho were crowded with people from all around. Zacchaeus decided to climb a sycamore tree so he wouldn't miss seeing Jesus as he passed by. Jesus wanted to see Zacchaeus too.

As Jesus passed through the city of Jericho, he spotted Zacchaeus high in a tree. Jesus stopped and asked him to come down because he wanted to go to his house. Zacchaeus came down and made Jesus welcome to go to his house. Zacchaeus told Jesus how he had cheated the people. He also said he would give half of his goods to the poor, for he was quite rich. He also promised Jesus that he would give back four times the amount of money he had gotten dishonestly. This was his way of saying "I'm sorry for my sins", to Jesus. Zacchaeus wanted to be right with Jesus. Jesus forgave him and he became a Christian that day. This can happen to us today.

Zacchaeus knew he hadn't been an honest tax collector. He knew that was not the right thing to do. So he told Jesus what he had done, he repented and became Jesus' friend. When we have done wrong, we can tell Jesus and he will forgive us too, and we can be his friend.

Discussion Questions

1. What would you have to do to get ready for Jesus to come to your house?

2. How can you become Jesus' friend?

Activity 1

Write the following phrase on the board: What if Jesus Came to Your House Today --. Give each child a sheet of paper and ask him/her to respond by describing what needs to be done before Jesus arrives.

Activity 2

Pass out drawing paper. Have children illustrate this story.

"Even so every good tree bringeth forth good fruit:
but a corrupt tree bringeth forth evil fruit:
(Matthew 7:17)

Good Fruit! Bad Fruit!

(Based on Matthew 7:18-19)

Jesus taught his disciples with little stories called parables. He once used a story about two trees, a *good* tree and a *bad* tree. Each tree produced its own kind of fruit.

Let's pretend these were apple trees. The *good* tree made nice, big, red juicy apples. The *bad* tree made tiny, hard, wormy apples. Which tree would you like to eat from? Of course we would all like the nice big, red, juicy apples! Jesus compared these trees and their fruit to us and the way we live.

Boys and girls that are obedient, kind, caring and honest could represent the good tree and its fruit. Some boys and girls are disobedient, dishonest, mean and hard to get along with. They could represent the bad tree and its fruit.

In his teachings, Jesus said "a tree is known by the fruit." Boys and girls are known by their actions. Their actions are just like the tree's fruit. Good fruit indicates a good tree. Good behavior indicates a good boy or girl. Jesus wants us to be bearers of good fruit – behavior. Bearing good fruit brings favorable consequences. Bearing bad fruit brings sadness, shame and punishment. What kind of fruit are you bearing?

Discussion Questions

1. What does a good apple look like?

2. What does a good apple taste like?

3. What does a good apple feel like?

4. How would you compare a good apple to a good boy or girl?

Activity

Use poster paper to make two trees. Put the trees on the bulletin board. Pass out red or yellow construction paper to each child. Instruct them to draw a good apple and a bad apple. Cut them out and attach them to the trees on the board (good on the good tree, and bad on the bad tree).

CHRIST BLESSING LITTLE CHILDREN.

"Remember now thou creator in the days of thy youth."
(Ecclesiastes 12:1)

Children Can Work for God

(Based on Ecclesiastes 12:1)

The Bible says, "Remember your creator while you are young, before the days of trouble come and the years come when you will say, 'I find no happiness in them'…"

As children we are full of energy and every part of our body works well. Our mind is sharp. We can think many wonderful things. We can remember stories, songs, games, and everything we need to have fun. Our eyes are strong and we can see well. Our ears are clear and we can hear well. Our mouth is full of good healthy teeth and we can eat anything we wish. Our legs are strong. We can walk, run and jump for hours without getting tired.

As we grow older, we have less energy. All of our body parts that use to work well begin to fail us. Our mind can't think and remember as well as it once did. Our eyes are dimmer. We might even need glasses. Our ears don't pick up sounds as well. We might need a hearing aid. Our teeth are decaying and we might need false teeth. Our legs are getting weak and we might need a walking cane. All the things our bodies once did well without problems have changed. We don't enjoy ourselves like we once did. We need to remember God while we are young. When we are young and full of energy and all of our body parts are working properly we can use them to do God's work. So invite Jesus to come and live in your heart while you are young and able to do what HE wants you to do. There are lots of jobs children can do for God.

Discussion Questions

1. What kind of jobs can children do to show they are working for God?

2. What kind of people can you help?

Activity

Allow children to play physical games such as: Tug of War, London Bridge, Tag, etc. They can also play sensory games like Pin the nose on the Clown, and Gossip. Place several items of different textures in a bag (call it a feely bag or touch bag) let children take turns touching and describing what was touched.

"Yet because this widow troubleth me, I will avenge her,
lest by her continual coming she weary me."
(Luke 18:5)

The Widow and the Unjust Judge

(Based on Luke 8:1-8)

Jesus used the story about a widow (a woman whose husband is dead) and the mean judge to teach us to pray and never give up.

In the story the judge was so mean that he didn't care about anyone – even God. The woman wanted her enemies to stop pestering her. She made trip after trip to the judge, begging for help. When the judge decided the woman was not going to give up asking for help, he finally granted her wish. Remember this was a very mean judge that cared only about himself. But the widow felt that if she would keep asking, he would finally grant her wish, and he did.

God is our loving Heavenly Father. He cares about us and everything that happens to us. However he wants us to make our requests known to him. He wants us to ask him to take care of our needs. Even when it seems like he is not listening, he wants us to keep asking. God is always listening and he knows what we need, but when we ask him for what we need and want, it shows that we honor him as our father.

If the mean old judge could finally say yes to the widow, then how much more can our loving Father answer our prayers? PRAY AND NEVER GIVE UP!

Discussion Questoins

1. How do we ask God for what we want or need?

2. What kind of things do you need or want from God?

3. What is a widow?

Activity 1

Allow children to respond to this question: What do you want God to do for you? Give each child a sheet of paper. Instruct them to write or draw what he/she wants from God.

Activity 2

Let children play "Mother may I". Choose a leader; let the other children line up across the room. The leader will call each child and give orders – example: Jimmy, take one baby step forward – Mary, take two giant steps backward. Keep playing until one of the children reaches the leader. He/she becomes the leader or can be eliminated.

"And Cain talked with Abel his brother, and it came to pass,
when they were in the field, that Cain rose up against
Abel his brother, and slew him."
(Genesis 4:8)

Jealousy Causes Pain

(Based on Genesis 4)

The first family was made up of Adam and Eve and their two sons, Cain and Abel. Cain and Abel were like you, they had assigned chores to do. Cain was responsible for taking care of the garden. Abel took care of the sheep. They each did their jobs well.

At last one day they brought offerings to the Lord. Cain brought some of his fruit as an offering, but not the best. Abel brought part of his first born best animals as his offering. The Lord was very pleased with Abel's offerings because he brought his best. He was not happy with Cain's offering because he did not bring his best. Cain felt angry. He was jealous because Abel pleased God and he didn't.

Cain asked Abel to go with him to the field one day. While they were in the field Cain attacked Abel and killed him. Then he had to be punished. Cain's jealousy had taken control and made him destroy his brother and himself.

The Bible tells us to do what is right. When we do what is right, the right thing takes control and we can be happy. God is also happy when we obey his word.

Discussion Questions

1. What does it mean to be jealous?

2. Could Cain have avoided being jealous of his brother? How?

3. Have you ever been jealous of someone? Did it make you want to harm that person?

Activitiy 1

Divide the children into groups of three. Give each group a dictionary. Appoint a writer, searcher, and a reporter. The writer will write what the searcher finds in the dictionary, the reporter will give a report of the findings. Have each group give examples of the definitions found in the report.

Activity 2

Let the children role play incidents showing jealousy. Examples: Someone in the group gets something new, makes a good grade, earn a treat etc.

"Jesus said unto him, 'It is written again thou shall not tempt the Lord thy God.'"
(Matthew 4:7)

Tempted

(Based on Matthew 4:1-10)

Have you ever been tempted to do the wrong thing? Did you yield (give in) to the temptation? Did you go ahead and do it? What does it mean to be tempted? You are tempted when you hear a voice inside tell you to do or say something that you know is wrong and you could get in trouble for. How can we not do what the voice says do?

Again, Jesus gave us an example. When He had fasted forty days and nights, the devil tried to get Jesus to turn stones into bread. Being very hungry he was tempted, but instead he ignored Satan. Satan did not give up. He tempted Jesus two more times. The last time Jesus told Satan to go away. He did not give in to him.

If we pray, we can also resist Satan. Satan, the devil is our enemy. We can overcome temptation by not listening to Satan, just as Jesus did. The voice that is trying to get us to say or do what is not right is the evil voice. We should not listen to it.

When you are tempted, pray and ask Jesus to help you to resist the temptations and he will.

Discussion Questions

1. Have you ever been tempted to do something wrong?

2. What do you think it means to be tempted?

3. Who can help you resist temptation?

Activity 1

Gather a variety of snack goodies (cookies, candy, nuts, etc.) Display these on the table on separate containers before class time. Instruct children not to touch any of the goodies until they are told. Watch to see who cannot resist the temptation. After the story has been read discuss temptation. Then let the children eat the snacks.

Activity 2

Cut to pieces of poster paper and mount them on the bulletin board or wall. Write "THINGS THAT TEMPT ME" on each piece of paper. Divide children into two groups. Give them a minute or two to write as many things as possible that is tempting on the piece of paper. Examples: taking money or other things, telling a lie, cheating on test, etc.

"And when they had bound him, they led him away, and
delivered him to Pontius Pilate, the governor."
(Matthew 27:2)

Just for You and Me

(Based on Matthew 27:1-5)

The people in charge long, long ago finally figured a way to accuse and kill Jesus. He had only been going to and fro working miracles and doing good among the people. The Roman Soldiers didn't like that. So they bound him up and carried him to the governor, Pontus Pilate, who found no fault in Him. This was the beginning of the suffering Jesus endured for you and me. Judas, one of his disciples turned his back on him and sold him for thirty pieces of silver. Jesus forgave him and still loved him. Judas soon realized what a terrible thing he had done. He was so guilty and ashamed he destroyed himself. How awful!

On the old rough and rugged cross, Jesus hung suffered and died just for you and me to have eternal life. He's coming back one day for his children who have chosen to obey him. What love he had for us!. He was spat upon, beaten and bruised just because he went about doing good – how cruel! He did it all for you and me to have a home in heaven. What love! Since he suffered, bled and died for us, let us live for him. We can ask him to forgive our sins and help us to obey his word and live with him forever.

Jesus was obedient to his father and suffered on the cross so mankind could have a right to the tree of life.

Discussion Questions

1. What can you do for Jesus?

2. What kind of things can you do that would be just like selling Jesus for thirty pieces of silver?

3. If you had been there, what do you think you could have done to help Jesus?

Activity 1

Use tag-board and cut a cross for each child. Let them use colored sand to cover the cross.

Activity 2

Encourage children to act out the story of Jesus' trip to Calvary, based on this story.

"And when he commanded the people to sit down on the ground: and he took seven loaves and gave thanks, and break and gave to his disciples to set before them: and did set them before the people and they had a few small fish and he blessed and commanded to set them also before them."
(Mark 8:6-7)

The Miracle Worker

(Based on Mark 8:1-10)

While Jesus was on earth he healed the sick, raised the dead and saved sinners. He also worked many miracles. Long, long ago a large group called a multitude was with Jesus. They had been with him for several days. Because they had been there so long they were very hungry. Jesus' disciples were near him. He said to them, "These people have been with me three days and they are hungry, and I must help them. I love them so much and don't want them to faint because they have no food.

Jesus' disciples asked a question, "How can a man satisfy these people here in the wilderness?" Jesus compassionately asked, "How many loaves do you have?" The answer was seven. Then Jesus with his miraculous power said, "Sit down everyone, men, women and children." He blessed the loaves and fish and there was more than enough for everyone, with seven baskets full left over. Four thousand people had been served. This was indeed one of Jesus' many miracles performed. He continued to work miracles as he traveled through the land. He is still working miracles today! When we wake up everyday, it is a miracle. When he saves us from our sins is another miracle. The list goes on and on. Jesus loves you dearly and he will work a miracle in your life if you trust him.

Discussion Questions

1. What is a miracle?

2. What miracle did Jesus perform in this story?

3. Why was that a miracle?

Activity

Give each child a piece of play dough and a plastic knife. Have them shape the play dough into a loaf of bread. Tell them to use the plastic knife to cut the bread into as many pieces as possible. Give a prize to the one with the most pieces.

Or

Use a Milky Way candy bar. Divide the children into groups of four. Give each group a candy bar. Have them work together to cut the candy bar into as many pieces as possible. Give a prize to the group with the most pieces. Then let them eat the candy.

"And he said, Verily I say unto you, except ye be converted, and
become as little children, ye shall not enter into the kingdom of heaven."
(Matthew 18:3)

Jesus Loves Children

(Based on Matthew 18:1)

"Who is the greatest in the Kingdom of Heaven?" Jesus' followers asked. They thought maybe it was one of them. But to their surprise, it was a little child! Children have certain innocence about them. They can disagree with one of their peers one minute and are friends again in the next minute. Children do not hold grudges against one another. They can readily forgive and move on. Children can also show humility easily. Jesus wants all of us to have such spirits. In order to enter heaven, we must have a child like attitude.

There was a time when children were forbidden to come to Jesus. Jesus said "Don't forbid them to come to me, for such is the Kingdom of Heaven." How precious is Jesus' love! Jesus also said to his followers, "If you want to be great in the Kindgom, become as a little child."

Children are important to Jesus and his Father God. Our entrance to heaven is base on having child like spirits. Jesus is hurt when someone hurts a child because they are so dear to him. "Jesus loves the little children, all the little children of the world."

Discussion Questions

1.   Who is the greatest in God's Kingdom?

2.   What attitude should we display to become a part of the kingdom?

3.   Why do you think Jesus loved children so much?

Activity 1

Cut a piece of blue poster paper, hang it on the wall. In the center of the poster paper, write "Jesus Love the Little Children". Let the children find and cut out pictures of children of different races and sizes from magazines. Instruct them to mount their pictures on the poster paper randomly.

Activity 2

Let the children listen to the song "Jesus Loves the Little Children". Allow then to sing along.

Saying, What wilt thou that I shall do unto thee? And he said, Lord,
that I may receive my sight. And Jesus said unto him,
Receive thy sight: thy faith hath saved thee.
(Luke 18:41-42)

A Blind Man Made Happy

(Based on Luke 18:35-43)

Can you imagine not having your eyesight at all? Just think about it, it must be miserable! There was a man in Bible time that had this problem. Not only was he blind, he was also a poor beggar. Alas one day he heard about Jesus passing through his city.

Jesus' trip to Jericho made the blind man very happy. He knew this was a chance for him to ask Jesus to help him. As the multitude of people passed him by, he made preparations to see Jesus. He cried in a loud voice, "Jesus, Jesus have mercy on me" repeatedly. The people tried to stop him, but he just got louder. He really wanted to receive his sight. Finally he got Jesus' attention. "Bring him to me", Jesus said. Jesus asked the man what he wanted. The blind man said, "I want to receive my sight." Jesus said, "Because you have believed, you have your sight." The man was so happy and thankful he went away rejoicing and praising God as he followed Jesus. He could now see what a good friend Jesus is!

You might not be physically blind, but if you have not accepted Jesus as your personal savior, you are spiritually blind. You can reach out to Jesus in prayer right now and ask him to give you spiritual sight and he will just as he gave the blind man his physical sight.

Discussion Questions

1. What does it mean to be blind?

2. How many kinds of blindness did the story mention?

3. Who is able to give sight to the blind?

Activity

Use a scarf for a blindfold. Let the children take turns being blindfolded and give different instructions. Let the children describe their feelings while blindfolded. Discuss with them how they would feel if they were really blind.

"And Moses stretched out his hand over the sea; and the Lord caused
the sea to go back by a strong east wind all that night, and
made the sea dry land, and the waters were divided."
(Exodus 14:21)

The Red Sea Miracle

(Based on Exodus 14:21-30)

Bedtime is story time in many households. When is story time at your house? One mom read one of the most exciting stories a child has ever heard. It was the story of how God parted the Red Sea. God is our creator and he can do all things, and he always takes care of his people.

Mom read how the Israelites, God's people had problems with a mean old King by the name of Pharaoh. God grew tired of the way he treated his people. "Enough", God said, "I'll put an end to this!"

God had given Pharaoh and his Egyptians enough time to go on with their business and leave his people alone, but he refused. God being all powerful had a plan. He caused the Red Sea water to split, making a dry path for the Israelites to pass through to escape the Egyptians. The Israelites arrived safely to the other side. As soon as the last Israelite crossed the sea, God allowed the water to come together again and Pharaoh and his army drowned.

One child said to the mom, "Oh mom, God can do anything. I can see how we need to respect and obey Almighty God: after all he owns the whole world!

Discussion Questions

1. Why did God split the Red Sea?

2. Who were God's children in this story?

3. How did he take care of them?

Activity

Fill a large clear plastic container with water. Let the children experiment with different objects to separate the water. Discuss what happens. Let the children discuss what probably happened when God split the Red Sea.

"In the beginning God created the heaven and the earth."
(Genesis 1:1)

The Power of God in Creation

(Based on Genesis 1)

God was in the beginning of time. Since he is all powerful, he decided one day to make a beautiful world.

In the beginning the world did not have any shape and it was dark. So God said, "Let there be light", and there was light. He saw his world getting more and more beautiful, so he decided to have darkness and light. It was called morning and evening. He called this the first day.

Water was everywhere. God decided to divide the waters from the waters. He called the upper part heaven and the lower part the sea. He placed sea creatures in the sea. In heaven he placed all the heavenly bodies, the sun, the moon, and the stars. He created the sun to rule the day and the moon and the stars to rule the night time. The dry land was called earth. On earth he placed fruit trees, grass, and other vegetation. He also created animals and other creatures to run around on earth. God saw everything he had made was good.

God knew earth was here to stay so he commanded the animals, birds and fish to reproduce its kind. He needed someone to rule the animals.

God said, "Let us make man in our own image." So God stooped down and got some clay and molded and shaped it into his mage and likeness. Then he blew the breath of life into man's nostrils. Man became a living soul. He named the first man Adam. Then he realized Adam was lonely. He caused Adam to fall asleep. While he was asleep God took a rib from his side and made Adam a helper and called her Eve. God created man to commune with him. All the other creation was made for man's use and enjoyment. God is powerful, all knowing and owns everything.

God gave the best gift the world has ever known, His son Jesus Christ. We can see his power in creation and we should never cease to praise him. His creation took six days and he rested on the seventh.

Discussion Questions

1. What does the word creation mean?

2. Name some of God's creation

3. Why did God make man?

4. What do you like most about the creation?

Activity 1

Create a scene with blue and green poster paper to resemble the earth and the sky. Let the children find and cut pictures from magazines and place them in the proper area on the poster paper, i.e. put trees and animals on the green, put the sun, moon, stars on the blue.

Activity 2

Give each child a piece of play dough, tell them to create something.

Answer Sheets

(Suggested answers to story questions. Children's answers should be similar to the suggested answers to be accepted.)

Story #1

1. Consequences mean something that happens because something else happened.

2. We should always obey all adults and others that have authority over us, and of course God.

3. Our serpent can be anything that gets in the way of doing what is right.

4. We should obey the soft still voice of God.

Story #2

1. Jesus taught us to be happy we must have a good attitude and build others up.

2. Our parents, teachers, pastor, Sunday School Teacher, and other adults can help us to learn what Jesus taught.

3. Attitude means how we feel about something or someone

Story #3

1. Jesus is the good shepherd

2. The good shepherd leads us to good things

3. We experience bad things when we don't follow the good shepherd

Story #4

1. To get ready for Jesus to come to my house, I would clean up really good. I would cook the best meal.

2. I can make Jesus my friend by accepting him as my savior.

Story #5

1. A good apple looks bright in color and shiny.

2. A good apple tastes juicy.

3. A good apple feels firm.

4. A good apple looks, feels, and tastes good. A good boy or girl looks and behaves well.

Story #6

1. Children can run errands for the elderly or handicapped to show they are working for God.

2. We can help homeless people, elderly people, handicapped people and lonely people.

Story #7

1. We talk to God in prayer to ask for what we need or want.

2. We need comfort, love, forgiveness, and assurance from God.

3. A widow is a woman whose husband has died.

Story #8

1. Jealously means feeling threatened by something or someone.

2. Yes, Cain could have avoided being jealous by loving and caring for his brother.

3. Yes, sometimes it makes me want to do harm. (Let the children feel free to discuss further).

Story #9

1. Yes, I have been tempted to do wrong.

2. I think being tempted means to want to do what is not the right thing to do really badly.

3. Jesus can help us resist temptation

Story #10

1. I can give my life to Jesus and live for him.

2. I can continue to do wrong things when I know to do better.

3. If I had been there I could have prayed for Jesus.

Story #11

1. A miracle is something that seems impossible to do.

2. Jesus fed a lot of people with a little food.

3. That was a miracle because it would have been impossible for an ordinary person to do.

Story #12

1. The greatest in God's kingdom is a little child.

2. We should have a humble attitude like a child.

3. Jesus loved children so much because they are innocent.

Story #13

1. To be blind means not able to see

2. The story mentioned two kinds of blindness, physically and spiritually.

3. Only Jesus can give sight to the blind

Story #14

1. God parted the Red Sea so the Israelites could escape the Pharaoh.

2. The Israelites were God's children in this story.

3. God took care of his children by protecting them from the Pharaoh.

Story #15

1. The word creation means to bring something new into existence.

2. God created the heavens and the earth, people, animals and birds.

3. God made man to worship him.

4. I like the creation of other people most.

Glossary

Attitude	How we feel about something or someone. This feeling could be good or bad.
Blind	Not being able to see.
Consequences	Something that happens because something else happened.
Creation	The act of bringing things into existence
Disobedience	Refusing to obey
Jealousy	Feeling threatened by something or someone.
Miracle	Something done that seemed impossible to do.
Pasture	A plot of land used for grazing cattle
Punishment	The act of causing pain for some wrong doing.
Shepherd	A man who tends and guards sheep
Temptation	Wanting to do what is not the right thing to do really badly.
Widow	A woman whose husband has died.

We are sure this book will be helpful for children as they grow up in today's society. It will teach them to shun the evil things and choose the good. This book can be used in Sunday school, Vacation Bible School or anywhere children need positive teaching.

"Even a child is known by his doings
whether they are pure or whether they are right." Proverbs 20:1

Printed in the United States
by Baker & Taylor Publisher Services